The text of this edition has been retold from the version by Joseph Jacobs.

Copyright © 2000 by Nord-Süd Verlag AG, Gossau Zürich, Switzerland
First published in Switzerland under the title *Hans und die Bohnenranke*
English text copyright © 2000 by North-South Books Inc.

First published in the United States, Great Britain, Canada,
Australia, and New Zealand in 2000 by North-South Books,
an imprint of Nord-Süd Verlag AG, Gossau Zürich, Switzerland.

Distributed in the United States by North-South Books Inc., New York.

Library of Congress Cataloging-in-Publication Data is available.
A CIP catalogue record for this book is available from The British Library.
ISBN 0-7358-1374-4 (trade binding)
1 3 5 7 9 TB 10 8 6 4 2
ISBN 0-7358-1375-2 (library binding)
1 3 5 7 9 LB 10 8 6 4 2
Printed in Belgium

For more information about our books, and the authors and artists
who create them, visit our web site: www.northsouth.com

Jack and the Beanstalk

An English Fairy Tale Retold by **Anthea Bell**

Illustrated by **Aljoscha Blau**

North-South Books · New York · London

ONCE UPON A TIME there was a poor widow who lived with Jack, her only son, and their cow.

Jack used to take the cow's milk to market every morning.

But one day the cow stopped giving milk, and the widow decided to sell her so that they could buy food.

So Jack set off to take the cow to market. On the way, they met a funny-looking man with a big black beard.

"Good morning, Jack," he said. "Where are you going?"

"Good morning," replied Jack, wondering how the man knew his name. "I'm going to market to sell our cow."

"Well," said the man, "you look like the right sort of fellow to sell cows! Can you tell me how many beans make five?"

"Two in each hand and one in your mouth," said Jack,
sharp as a tack.

"Right," said the man, and he took some strange-looking
beans out of his pocket. "I'll exchange these beans for your
cow! You think that sounds like a bad bargain? Ah, but you
don't know what kind of beans they are. Just plant them
overnight, and they'll grow up to the sky by morning!"

"It's a deal!" said Jack.

So Jack went home with the beans, feeling pleased with himself, but his mother was very angry with him for giving away her cow.

"Take that!" she said, hitting him. "And that, and that!" Then she threw the beans out of the window into the garden and sent Jack to bed without any supper.

Jack was sorry that his mother was so upset, and he fell asleep feeling miserable.

But during the night the beans out in the garden split and began to grow into a huge beanstalk, twining up past the window and right into the clouds.

When Jack woke up the next morning he
saw the wonderful beanstalk. "The old man
was telling the truth after all!" he cried happily.
He climbed straight out of the window and
up the beanstalk, up and up into the sky.
There he met a gigantic woman who seemed
to be expecting him.

"Good morning, ma'am," said Jack, very
politely. "Would you be kind enough to give
me some breakfast?"

"You'll be breakfast yourself if you don't
get away from here," said the woman. "My
husband the ogre likes nothing better
than broiled boys on toast."

"I may as well be broiled as die of hunger!"
said Jack. "Do please give me something to eat!"

"Oh, very well, my lad," said the ogre's wife.
"Come into the kitchen with me." And she
gave him some bread and cheese and milk.

It wasn't long before the ogre came home, with his feet going thump, thump, thump!

Quick as lightning, the woman bundled Jack into the oven. As soon as the ogre was inside the house, he flared his nostrils like a horse, and bellowed:

Fee-fi-fo-fum,
I smell the blood of an Englishman.
Be he alive, or be he dead,
I'll grind his bones to make my bread!

"Nonsense," said his wife. "You must be smelling the scraps of that little boy you had for supper yesterday. Sit down and eat your breakfast, do!"

When the ogre had finished his breakfast he yawned, and then he took some bags of gold coins out of a chest and began counting the money. As he counted he fell asleep, and shook the whole house with his snoring.

Then Jack crept out of the oven on tiptoe, picked up one of the bags of gold, ran out of the house, and started down the beanstalk. He threw the bag of gold into his mother's garden, where it landed with a thud, and Jack himself was soon down after it and in the widow's arms.

"Well, wasn't I right about those magic beans?" he said, giving her the gold.

So they lived comfortably on the ogre's gold for some time.

When the gold was all gone, Jack decided to
try his luck at the top of the beanstalk again, and
he climbed cheerfully up it and into the clouds.

He went to the ogre's house, and found the
gigantic woman standing on the doorstep. "Aren't
you the boy who came here before?" she said.
"What do you know about my husband's missing
bag of gold?"

"Give me something to eat, and I'll tell you," said Jack.

Well, the woman was curious, so she put a plate full
of food in front of him. But Jack had hardly begun
to eat before the ogre came striding into the
house again, thump, thump, thump, shouting:

Fee-fi-fo-fum,
I smell the blood of an Englishman.
Be he alive, or be he dead,
I'll grind his bones to make my bread!

Jack hid in the oven once more, and when the ogre had finished his breakfast Jack heard him tell his wife, "Bring me the hen that lays the golden eggs."

The ogre only had to say "Lay!" and the hen laid a golden egg every time.

Soon the ogre fell asleep again, snoring—and Jack snatched up the wonderful hen and stole out of the house and away.

But the cackling of the hen woke the ogre. However, his wife soon calmed him down.

When Jack was home he showed his mother the wonderful hen, and said, "Lay!" The hen laid egg after golden egg.

The beanstalk was still growing up to the sky, and Jack was tempted to try his luck again. This time he didn't go into the ogre's house but hid behind a bush outside, and when the ogre's wife went to fetch water he slipped in and climbed into the big copper cauldron used for boiling the laundry.

Soon the woman came back with the ogre, who was crying out:

Fee-fi-fo-fum,
I smell the blood of an Englishman.
Be he alive, or be he dead,
I'll grind his bones to make my bread!

"If it's that rascal who stole your bag of gold and the hen that lays the golden eggs," said the woman, "he's sure to be hiding in the oven."

But when she opened the oven, nothing but ashes fell out.

The ogre searched the whole place—in the chest, under the table—but luckily for Jack he didn't look inside the copper cauldron.

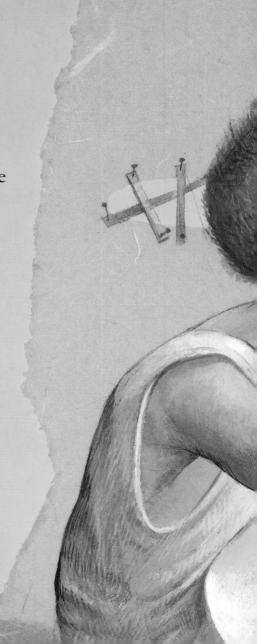

After breakfast the ogre called,
"Wife, bring me my golden harp!"
As soon as it was in front of him
the ogre said, "Sing, harp!" and
the harp sang soft, sweet music.

It went on singing until the ogre
was fast asleep and snoring.

Then Jack crept out of hiding,
crawled over to the table, caught
hold of the harp and ran off.
But the harp called out, "Master!
Master!" and woke the ogre, who
came running after Jack and would
have caught him, only Jack had
a good start and soon reached the
beanstalk. Then he began climbing
down.

"Master! Master!" cried the harp once again, but Jack shouted to his mother even louder, "Mother, bring me a hatchet, quick!"

As he jumped to the ground he seized the hatchet, swung it, and began chopping down the beanstalk.

The beanstalk quivered and shook as the ogre came closer.

Another chop of the hatchet, and the great beanstalk swayed. Then the ogre fell down and broke his crown, and the beanstalk came toppling after.

Then Jack gave his mother the golden harp,
and what with showing it and selling the
golden eggs they became very rich
and lived happily ever after.